To the real Shane and our babies.
—A.L.A.

To my son, Caiden—I hope Shane inspires you to
relentlessly chase after your dreams, dance with your
heart, and show pride in your West Indian heritage.
—S.K.J.

Farrar Straus Giroux Books for Young Readers
An imprint of Macmillan Publishing Group, LLC
120 Broadway, New York, NY 10271
mackids.com

Our books may be purchased in bulk for promotional, educational, or business use. Please
contact your local bookseller or the Macmillan Corporate and Premium Sales Department
at (800) 221-7945 ext. 5442 or by email at MacmillanSpecialMarkets@macmillan.com.

Library of Congress Control Number: 2021058425

First edition, 2023
Book design by Mina Chung
Color separations by Bright Arts (H.K.) Ltd.
Printed in China by Toppan Leefung Printing Ltd., Dongguan City, Guangdong Province

ISBN 978-0-374-38994-9
1 3 5 7 9 10 8 6 4 2

BIG TUNE

RISE OF THE DANCEHALL PRINCE

ALLIAH L. AGOSTINI

ILLUSTRATED BY
SHAMAR KNIGHT-JUSTICE

Farrar Straus Giroux
New York

IT'S THE WEEKEND, first in June;
speaker's blasting out big tune!

Cousins, aunties, uncles, friends
pack the house, and fun begins.

Eating jerk pork, drinking Ting.
Sweat drops down as people sing.
Swaying hips wine fast and slow.
Brown skin shines with black light's glow.

Shane grabs cans,
his favorite chore.

Five cent, ten cent,
dolla, more.
Getting close to his end goal,
high-tops with a pump-up sole.

"Shane's so shy, and he can't dance!"
brothers tease, don't know his plans.

He keeps focused on the prize,
blocks their shouts, and rolls his eyes.

Soon he sneaks up to his room.
Presses play, then grabs a broom.

Out of everybody's sight,
Shane could dance and sing all night!

He can dance, but just won't try.
Pressure's high—he's terrified!

Daddy is the dancehall king.

Dance so cool and even sing!

Shane heads out, big dreams in mind.
Picked up each can he could find.

He's been saving for a year;
five more bucks, then kicks are here!

He dances when no one's around,
plays big tune and pumps the sound.

Running Man,   then hits a split!

Oh, this crowd can't handle it!!

Every day his moves get hotta.
Ends them with a shout to

SHABBA!

Now first weekend of July.
Bashment canceled?! Shane asks why.
"Music done! The speaker's blown."
Shane lets out the biggest groan.

Every face is hanging low.
No one speaks, just eating slow.
Daddy sulks and Mommy's sad,
siblings pout. The mood's so bad!

Shane goes upstairs, checks his stash:
almost ninety dollars cash.

"Be right back." He disappears,
pushes pedals, works the gears.

Shane heads toward a nearby store,
buys the speaker by the door.
"Can you bring it right away?
Today is Big Tune Saturday!"

Shane comes back with a surprise.
Round the table, smiles rise.
"Call the aunties, call each friend.
Let's tun' up, let fun begin!"

"Yes, come through, the party's on!
Bring yourselves, we'll play your song.

Likkle Shane found a quick fix.
Used cash saved to buy new kicks!"

Friends and family soon pour in,

selector hype, records spin.

Swaying hips wine fast and slow.
Brown skin shines with black light's glow.

Shane's the champ! They pass a hat,
fill it up, and just like that . . .
over ninety dollars raised!
Even brothers offer praise.

What a Big Tune Saturday!
All Shane's shyness melts away.
Grabs the mic to sing and dance,
princely with his dancehall stance.

$ 5 $

Sings and sways, wines fast and slow,
crowd is rocking, feels the flow!
Brown skin shines with black light's glow.

Brown skin shines with black light's glow.

AUTHOR'S NOTE

Family, friends, music, food, and drink are a universal recipe for a good time! And in immigrant communities like the early 1990s Brooklyn, New York, Jamaican community depicted here, parties or bashments are an opportunity to reconnect with local family, friends, and the rhythm and flavors of a home thousands of miles away.

There's nothing like the taste of sweet and tart grapefruit Ting soda, the smoky spicy flavor of anything jerked and grilled to perfection, the warmth of hugs and laughter, and the booming sound of a giant speaker while a selector plays big tune (pronounced big *CHune*), the top hits. Because at family parties if the music's right, almost everybody dances . . . however they best can.

Anyone can dance to Jamaican dancehall, whether they put their fingers up and rhythmically bend over backward to bogle (pronounced *BOHgul*), slowly move their hips in a circle and wine, do their best to sway to the rhythm of the music, or try any of the countless other dancehall moves that originated with dance crews in Jamaica and made their way overseas.

But not everyone can be a Dancehall King or Queen—that title is reserved for the very best dancers of all.

Ska, rocksteady, reggae, and dancehall are just some of the musical styles that originated and evolved in the tiny but well-known island nation of Jamaica. Dancehall music is one of the most contemporary, also known for its signature dances and influence on American mainstream. It emerged as an up-tempo offshoot of reggae in the late 1970s and crossed over into American mainstream in the 1980s to early 1990s as dancehall riddims (rhythms) fused with hip-hop and R&B. Shabba Ranks, Chaka Demus & Pliers, Super Cat, and Patra were some of the most popular artists to cross over in the early 1990s, with more to come as the decade rolled on.

First-generation American children often stay plugged into the cultural traditions of their or their parents' birthplace while also keeping up with and ultimately influencing American popular culture. Plenty of musical artists boast Caribbean—and specifically Jamaican—roots, including Clive Campbell, better known as DJ Kool Herc, the founding pioneer of hip-hop; the Notorious B.I.G.; Heavy D; Busta Rhymes; and Sandra "Pepa" Denton of Salt-N-Pepa, all artists who ultimately made big tune of their own.

MAR 2023